ICCUP

A SECOND IS

A Child's Book of Time

by Hazel Hutchins

Illustrated by

Kady MacDonald Denton

ARTHUR A. LEVINE BOOKS

AN IMPRINT OF SCHOLASTIC INC.

A HICCUP

How long is a second?

A second is a hiccup—

The time it takes to kiss your mom

Or jump a rope
Or turn around.

How long is a minute?

Sixty seconds to a minute,
Sixty hiccups, sixty hops.

Or if you sing just one small song
Chorus, verses, not too long

That's just enough to fill
A minute.

How long is an hour?

Sixty minutes singing by.
If you build a sandy tower

Run right through a sprinkly shower
Climb a tree and smell a flower
Pretend you have a secret power
That should nicely fill
An hour.

How long is a day?

Twenty-four hours by the clock.
Starting when the sun comes up
A day needs filling, like a cup
Hiccups, kisses, songs and showers
Lots of trees and lots of flowers

Breakfast, lunch and snack and dinner
Play some games and cheer the winner
Draw a picture, read a book
Tell a joke and learn to cook
Watch the sunshine fade away
Fall asleep, and that's a day!

How long is a week?

Seven days all in a line.
Sunday Monday Tuesday Wednesday
Thursday Friday and the end day
Saturday—a favorite one!
Some are quiet, some are fun.

Work days, home days, play days, school days

Seven wake-ups, seven sleeps

Close your eyes and do not peek
But you'd never
Ever ever
Stay asleep for one whole week.

How long is a month?

Four weeks add up to form a month.
Lots of time for things to change
Seasons often rearrange

Winters melt and warm to springs
Caterpillars find their wings
And if you fall and scrape a shin
In a month there's brand-new skin

Learn to tie your laces tight

Learn to float, relaxed and light

Learn to count clean up to ten
Learn to count back down again

Watch the moon grow round and fat
Then thin again, imagine that!
And all of it in one month flat.

How long is a year?

Twelve months together make a year.
A great big circle spinning round
Climb aboard, you're one year bound

You'll grow right out of your old shoes
And taller too—now that's good news!

Sunshine, snow and rain and squall

Winter, spring, summer, fall

Twigs on trees grow leaves and peaches

See how far a whole year reaches

Tiny babies learn to walk
Bigger babies learn to talk
Holidays of every kind
Linked together in a line

When your birthday's almost here,
You are older
By a year!

Changes come and changes go
Round and round the years you'll grow

Till you're bigger, till you're bolder
Till you're ever so much older.

And through all the hours and days
As time unfolds in all its ways
You will be loved—

As surely as
A second is a hiccup.

For the great-grandchildren
of Peggy and Bill Sadler,
a delightful, ever-growing circle.
— H. H.

For Eila. — K. M. D.

Text copyright © 2004 by Hazel Hutchins
Illustrations copyright © 2004, 2007 by Kady MacDonald Denton

Library of Congress Cataloging-in-Publication Data

Hutchins, H. J. (Hazel J.)
A second is a hiccup : a child's book of time / by Hazel Hutchins ;
illustrated by Kady MacDonald Denton.
— 1st American ed.   p. cm.
ISBN-13: 978-0-439-83106-2
ISBN-10: 0-439-83106-7
1. Time—Juvenile literature. 2. Time measurements—Juvenile literature.
I. Denton, Kady MacDonald, ill. II. Title. QB209.5.H88 2007   529—dc22   2006007561

10 9 8 7 6 5 4 3 2   07 08 09 10 11

Printed in Singapore   46
First American edition, March 2007

Book design by Elizabeth B. Parisi